### BOOK REVIEW

*The pages of colorful, confused
ducks would tickle most small
children and make a wonderful
read-aloud story.*

from S C H O O L   L I B R A R Y   J O U R N A L

Weekly Reader Children's Book Club presents

# FOLLOW ME!

### written and illustrated by
## MORDICAI GERSTEIN

WILLIAM MORROW AND COMPANY
New York • 1983

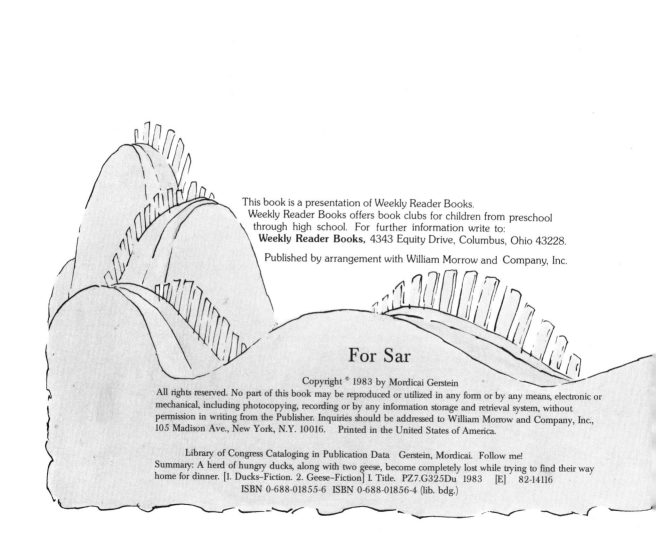

This book is a presentation of Weekly Reader Books.
Weekly Reader Books offers book clubs for children from preschool
through high school. For further information write to:
**Weekly Reader Books,** 4343 Equity Drive, Columbus, Ohio 43228.

Published by arrangement with William Morrow and Company, Inc.

## For Sar

Copyright © 1983 by Mordicai Gerstein
All rights reserved. No part of this book may be reproduced or utilized in any form or by any means, electronic or
mechanical, including photocopying, recording or by any information storage and retrieval system, without
permission in writing from the Publisher. Inquiries should be addressed to William Morrow and Company, Inc.,
105 Madison Ave., New York, N.Y. 10016. Printed in the United States of America.

Library of Congress Cataloging in Publication Data   Gerstein, Mordicai.   Follow me!
Summary: A herd of hungry ducks, along with two geese, become completely lost while trying to find their way
home for dinner. [1. Ducks–Fiction. 2. Geese–Fiction] I. Title. PZ7.G325Du 1983   [E]   82-14116
ISBN 0-688-01855-6  ISBN 0-688-01856-4 (lib. bdg.)

A yellow duck was walking along the road.
He was hungry and in a hurry to get home.

After a while he met a blue duck.
"Hello," said the blue duck.
"Where are you going in such a hurry?"

"Home," said the yellow duck.
"It's almost dinner time."
"You're going the wrong way,"
   said the blue duck. "Home is that way."

"Are you sure?" asked the yellow duck.

"Follow me," said the blue duck.

After a while they met a red duck.
"Hello," said the red duck.
"Where are you two going?"

"Home," said the yellow duck.
"Dinner," said the blue duck.
"Why are you going west?" asked the red duck.
"Home is east. Follow me."

"Are you sure?" asked the yellow duck.
"Follow him," said the blue duck,
    pointing to the red duck.

"Walk this way," said the red duck.

So they did, and after a while they met a green duck.
"Hello," said the green duck.
"Do you know how to get home?"

"It's this way," said the yellow duck.
"Are you sure?" asked the green duck.
"Yes," said the red duck.
"No," said the blue duck.

"I'm hungry," said the yellow duck.
"Let's follow her," said the blue duck,
  pointing to the green duck.

"Hurry!" said the green duck.

After a while they met a big purple goose.
"Watch out!" he said.
"I'm a big purple goose in a hurry to get home."

"We're ducks," said the green duck.
"We're hurrying home too," said the blue duck.
"We're walking this way," said the red duck.

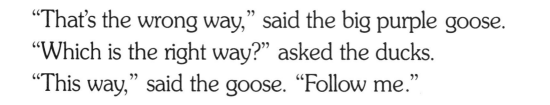

"That's the wrong way," said the big purple goose.
"Which is the right way?" asked the ducks.
"This way," said the goose. "Follow me."

"Follow him!" said the green duck.
"Hurry!" said the red duck.
"Don't push!" said the yellow duck.
"Are we there yet?" asked the blue duck.

Along came an orange goose and a black duck.
"Where are you going?" asked the black duck.
"We're lost!" said the blue duck.

"Are you all ducks?" asked the orange goose.
"All except for him," said the green duck,
    pointing to the purple goose.

"But we're all completely lost!" said the yellow duck.
"Lost! Lost! Lost!" they all said.

"Let's stop and clean our feathers,"
said the red duck. "It may help."
"Or it may not," said the orange goose.

While they were busy cleaning their feathers,
along came a duckherd.

"Hello, ducks. Hello, geese.
Are you hungry?" he asked.

"Quack. Quack. Quack. Quack.
Honk. Honk. Quack," they answered.

"Are you in a hurry?" he asked them.

"Quack. Quack. Quack. Quack.
Honk. Honk. Quack," they answered.

"Would you like to come home to dinner?"
he asked them.

"Quack. Quack. Quack. Quack. Honk. Honk. Quack," they answered.

"Follow me!" said the duckherd.
  And off they went, this color and that color,
    walking this way and that way,
    quacking and honking,
    all hungry and hurrying all the way...

. . . home.